The Tenth Life

The Tenth Life

Michael Titus
and
Brett Fernau

leaf~litter!Press

The Tenth Life

ISBN: 978-0615556192

First edition: November 2011
leaf~litter!Press
leaflitterpress@yahoo.com

Printed in the U.S.A.

For all those not-yet-adopted animals
in lonely shelters, waiting for their forever homes.

Contents

The Tenth Life

Based on a true story.

Chapter One

Transition

All right. Well, then. What's next? Where do I go from here?

That sums up what I was thinking after I realized that there was something to this idea of reincarnation—or at least some form of afterlife. I was looking at the odd remnant I knew was me and it was dead. I remembered my last breath and the panic I felt when I was unable to draw another one. Then, no darkness. No light to go toward. No harps, angels, accordions—or vast, spindrift nebulae to inhabit or to bear witness to. Here I was and there *it* was. And it was dead and I was not. It was that simple.

All I felt at the moment was total confusion. This whole "lingering on" business was not at all what I'd expected. When you're dead, you're dead. That's it. Right? End of story. The thought is bred into us that we only have this one dear and precious life and we are to greet each day as if we wouldn't be lucky enough to see another. I was never one to hold out any hope of going to heaven or Valhalla or paradise. Or anywhere else for that matter.

And yet here I was. Am. I still exist but as…what? A ghost,

haunting only myself? A soul, waiting for some celestial traffic light to turn green? A wandering collection of still-firing brain cells, a memory not quite faded into the inevitable oblivion? I wondered how much time I had left before *Nothing* approached and waved me away with an indifferent, skeletal hand.

Whatever I was, I was still alive. At least in the sense that I could think about these matters. And I could remember everything, including dying. The question remained: what now? It felt like the first day at a new job. Only more so. All I could do was hover and try to learn. But I had no supervisor. It appeared that I wasn't going to be assigned a spirit guide. I didn't have to punch a time clock, but would gladly have done so. That would at least be a physical action, some semblance of doing something like work. Better than not knowing or doing anything at all. I loomed, therefore I was.

But any action other than hovering was denied me. I hovered above what I had thought was me. Once I accepted the fact that whatever I was, I wasn't a dead body...I felt fear. It was almost a delightful moment, because it was a sensation. Fear was something to feel, to know. I began to ponder heaven and hell again. But nothing happened to me. I just hovered until some hospital staff came and took my body away.

Still, nothing happened. My old tired shell of a body was gone. I, whatever *I* was now, remained. A lot of people get struck by lightning and survive. I was one of them. I just did not survive within my body. I don't even remember getting illuminated by the sky's crooked finger of fire. It happened in an instant. In a similar instant, I felt...alone.

Fear was one thing. Fear fades. Loneliness was like a map with all the spatial data erased. Direction was blank. A page with no words. A white-out in a snow-fisted wilderness. It was a childhood with distant, indifferent parents. I was lonely because

I was still *something.* It would have been better to be nothing at all, to fade into oblivion.

I looked around the hospital room. I tried to see myself, any part of myself, but there was nothing to see. I stared at the floor. I tried to speak but couldn't utter a sound. Not a squeak or a tiny moan. I had no chains to rattle, like Marley's ghost. I was only equipped with icy silence. What did I expect? People to point and shriek and run hither and thither?

Someone came into the room and began to pack up the hospital bed and the medical gear that had been used to tend to the needs of my ailing body. I tried to ask them a question. I shouted at them, struck out at them with all the invisible fury I could muster. Without a body I had no way to interact, no possibility to communicate. I had a dim memory of poltergeists and experienced a fervent desire to brood and command solid objects to zip across the room like disturbed hornets. Or even just to hear myself scream. I hovered for a long time. I don't know how long. I didn't really care. People came into the room and left. The room was cleaned, my meager furnishings moved out, some other unhealthy was body moved in and connected to tubes and wires. Machines blinked and nurses flocked. I paid little attention to any of this new movement below.

Time is a puzzle when you are "dead." A puzzle with no pieces. A river of ice. I do not know how long I hovered over the room my body once occupied. It might have been a minute, an hour, a day—or eternity. At this point, the distinctions had vanished. Eventually there came a point in this non-linear framework where I knew I was…bored.

Since there was nothing forthcoming to change my static situation, I tried to will myself beyond this first death to some secondary cessation. I failed. I assumed I had arrived at some preordained forever, looming in this room until time and space itself ended like the collapse of the Big Bang. But I could not accept this. My very sanity was at stake.

What could I do? Perhaps I could...move. But how? I had no body to marshal into action. No legs to scissor myself in any direction. Could I move at all? I realized I hadn't made an attempt at this. I hadn't cared to try.

What if I just decided to be *over there*? I did. I was. This was extraordinary! I couldn't feel myself move, yet I knew I had. That meant that hope existed, in whatever capricious form it had taken. I could move! So I did. I moved all over the room. Then I moved outside the building and was overwhelmed and nearly lost. It was too much, too big, too soon. If I still possessed a body, I'd be in excruciating pain! It was like phantom nerves exploding, although I had no nerves and was unclear yet about being a phantom. But I *was*. Though death had claimed me, it had not revealed any secrets or instructions. I needed to catch my breath, if you'll forgive that phrase.

After a bit of practice I found that I could orient myself to the larger space if I only looked in one direction at a time. It was easier if I decided where I was going first and then went just that far and stopped. I discovered that I could control where I was going and my fear of becoming even more lost receded. I was cautious until I gained a measure of confidence in my ability to arrive at my intended destination. And then I traveled.

I could see and get some sensation of the sound of things. I could somehow sense the conversations of people but I was removed from them, still an outsider. I could not get them to notice *me*. It was frustrating. But it was better to be thwarted than to be completely helpless. So I traveled. Everywhere.

In my immeasurable wanderings, I saw much of this earth. I witnessed births. I was present at deaths, though these did not bring me the comrades I'd longed for. I saw temples and ramshackle huts, love and betrayal, the alchemy of photosynthesis, the flowering of forsythia from cast seed. I visited the Earth's elders—the Bristlecone Pines, the Cypress, the Sequoias. And Methuselah, a tree nearly 5000 years old.

I imagined my dead shadow crossing the full sherbet-orange moon like a witch on a broomstick. I sensed coral grow in the ocean and saw, in the depths, unnamed aquatic denizens give fuel to bioluminescence to find prey. Mountains. Valleys. Peaks and gorges. Flora and fauna. And lightning. Yes, I watched heaven's cutlery excel in such brightness! It was all glorious.

I traveled much. I could voyage far and wide. And yet, something was missing. I'd seen the grand game of life, and here I was sitting on the sidelines. I longed to participate. I lusted after purpose. I realized that there were things I needed to do, ways in which I could help. But how? How to get back in the game?

Just when I began to despair, I was called back.

Chapter Two

Mr. Vorbec

A tall man slowly made his way down the corridor that led to his apartment. He was dressed in a somewhat worn suit, a woolen vest, solid red tie and a brand new brown fedora, from which long wisps of unkempt white hair emerged. His limp was almost imperceptible. He didn't shuffle but his measured gait, long acquired, was made noticeable only by the fact that upon his feet were a pair of burgundy house slippers.

He stopped at his door and fished in his trousers for his keys. He slid them around the key-ring, savoring the design, texture and weight of each one. He loved keys. He kept a useless skeleton key on the ring because it was unique and old. Just like he was. When the correct key came into view, his lips curled in a wisp of a smile. Before he could put the key into the lock, his hand began to tremble and he dropped the key ring.

"Son of a bitch," he murmured. The old man groaned as he bent over to pick them up. He found the right key again, inserted it into the lock and let himself in.

Mr. Edward Vorbec was home.

Closing the door behind him, he took off his hat, placed it on a coat rack and surveyed his domain. His cat, Bwca, who had been enjoying a sliver of evening sunlight on the window ledge, stretched, sat up and surveyed the only human it tolerated in *his* domain. Man and cat glared at each other for a few moments and then the man walked over, petted the cat and reached into his pocket for the cat-treats he'd ventured outside to purchase.

The cat cocked its head. The man mimicked this action. Then the man opened the package and deposited several treats onto the windowsill. The cat sniffed them carefully and then began to eat them one by one, purring with contentment. The man had done well.

"That's all for you. At least for tonight," said Mr. Vorbec. "Enjoy! Somebody might as well." He turned away and went into the kitchen to make himself a cup of tea.

Bwca watched him leave the living room with a look of disdain. *Tea again*, he thought. *More habitual than I am.*

When Mr. Vorbec returned, he stood like a broken statue, tea and saucer in hand, and surveyed his life once again. His life was contained in this one room. It was a cozy place. It was filled with all the things he admired. The walls were covered with original art, most of it strange and vintage. A boy with insect wings raised outward from his shoulders. A wizened fat man with blue smoke evaporating from his bald dome. An old woman sitting in a wicker chair with a dinosaur skeleton sneaking up behind her. Twin little girls in Victorian dress standing beside a large grasshopper; one of the twins holding a skeleton key. This one was his personal treasure. Eerie things, yet not without a nod and a wink of humor.

There was much clutter. All manner of books filled the wooden wall-cases, overflowing onto the floor. Books were also piled up in stacks around his armchair and sofa. Mr. Vorbec didn't mind the clutter. "What the hell," he'd say. He was 87 years old. Alone except for the cat. He could live in whatever manner suited him. He'd earned that right.

He sat down in his cozy armchair and sipped his tea. He'd hardly replaced the cup in the saucer when his old rotary phone rang. The nonsensical machine did this once or twice a day. He never answered it because he didn't know anyone and had no inclination to make a new acquaintance. He wasn't sure why he'd never just had the damned thing disconnected. He permitted his antagonist to ring twice before he picked up the receiver and slammed it immediately back into its cradle.

"Hello and Goodbye again!" he shouted into the room. Bwca yawned. He'd heard this a hundred times before and was bored with the performance. The cat was old. The Man was old. The apartment was old. The whole place reeked to the cat of endings. But he played his part, this cat. Bwca stayed out of the way as much as possible.

Mr. Vorbec twisted in his chair to get comfortable. His back hurt. His hip ached. The truth was he was wracked with pains—large and small. He'd given up on the "quacks," as he called the doctors that he used to see on quite a regular basis. He'd decided to watch what was left of his life play out without their intervention, their tests, their probing, their plotting. Or anyone else's for that matter. After his last appointment, two years ago, the receptionist attempted to hand him a card with the date of his next visit penned in. He'd told her, in front of his doctor— and the rest of the staff—to "piss off."

As Mr. Vorbec sipped his tea, he made a small mewling sound of delight.

Bwca watched the Man and listened with a renewed interest. The cat knew the man better than the man knew himself. Cats always do. For the most part, they aren't all that curious about humans. Bwca was different. He had to feign the typical elderly and expected feline indifference. He did not sleep with the man. He acted as if he merely tolerated the man's presence. He'd stopped being a lap cat ages ago. But Bwca kept an eye on the man. He could not be underfoot so as to cause the man to fall. The man was now far too unsteady as it was. If he fell, he'd end up in one of those human shelters, from which there would be no return.

And Bwca could not permit such a thing to happen. Not until…

Briiiing briiiiiiinggg. The phone again. It rarely rang twice in one day.

"Hell's Bells!" exclaimed Mr. Vorbec with a sudden lunge out of the chair. He grabbed the phone, slammed it on the side table until Bwca thought it would shatter. When it had gone silent, the man ran his mottled hands through his wild white hair and then brushed away the sweat on his forehead with a sleeve. He slumped back down into his chair, panting, too tired to retain much anger anymore.

Bwca watched this with alarm. *Am I too late? Have I grown so complacent that I forgot my purpose here?* The cat knew it was time to act. It was now or never. He slid off the windowsill and approached the man. He began to rub his sleek black body across the man's shins, meowing.

"What's this?" asked Mr. Vorbec. "What the devil has got into you, Cat?"

Bwca continued to sadly vocalize, rub, purr. He tried to make his cat-voice as plaintive as possible. The man was perplexed. Bwca was a companion who sat in the corner, was fed, watered and given treats. Nothing more, nothing less. The man admired him, in his own distant way, but he and the cat had an implicit understanding: you go your way, I'll go mine. This new and quirky behavior was breaking that pact.

But Bwca persisted.

Finally, Mr. Vorbec picked the cat up with a groan from his aching joints and placed him on the ottoman opposite him. The cat looked at him strangely with incandescent yellow eyes. It was almost a frightening glare. A staring contest, which the man had no chance of winning. Bwca groomed his paw briefly and then began to meow like a lone wolf howling at the round lozenge of moon beyond the curtains. Mr. Vorbec looked on, amazed. Bwca pawed the air. Then he leaped off the ottoman and ran into the bedroom.

"So what? So now I'm not good enough for you, you ungrateful wretch!"

Bwca came back and began the rubbing process all over again. And again, Mr. Vorbec picked him up and sat him on the ottoman. The cat pawed the air again.

"You want to play, eh?" the man questioned. Bwca meowed, still pawing the air. Mr. Vorbec thought he detected some odd smile, if that was the correct word, on the cat's face.

"Well, forget it! You're old. I'm old. We don't play! Go use the litter box so I can clean it before bedtime. Off now! Shoo!" But Bwca would not shoo. He winked at the man. *You call me cat. You have called me cat for years. Speak my real name, man. Call me by name, Vorbec. Call me by my…name.*

Mr. Vorbec, his tea now cold, turned away from those terrible, lovely cat eyes. He put his hands over his ears, in a vain attempt to drown out the sound of the cat's voice. He thought he had suddenly lost his mind, become senile. He knew how all his days flowed, without a great deal of unexpected interruption. He could not bear much change in his routine. It was unsettling. It was wrong, wasn't it? It had been…but now? The man dropped his hands to his sides. The cat fell silent, but still…smiled. It dawned on the man that this was a most human expression. And that was unacceptable.

"What do you want?" yelled Mr. Vorbec. "What is it that you need that you don't have here now?"

The cat continued smiling. It was grotesque, thought the man.

"Well, bugger off!"

The cat began to chase its tail. It Then it jumped, as if to capture an invisible moth. *Say my real name. Say my real name. There is one thing left to do, but you must utter my name! I do this for you, Vorbec. The choice is yours.*

The man slowly calmed down, drained from this apoplectic adventure thrust suddenly into his small, cozy existence. He sighed and drained the rest of his tea, not even realizing that it was tepid.

"Well, you want to play. I don't play. I suppose I can go out tomorrow and find another cat. The two of you can do as you please. But leave me out of it!" Mr. Vorbec rose with more groans and headed toward the bedroom. He was exhausted. "Tomorrow then. But no promises." The cat purred as the man practically stumbled through the bedroom doorway. The man turned on the light. Before he shut the door, he turned.

"Good night, Cat."

Chapter Three

Quint

———❦———

I needed to be able to interact with someone or some…thing. I wanted to touch something, anything at this point, and feel the texture. I missed sensations; the tastes and smells and feelings that I had when I inhabited my old body.

Would it be possible to get another body? How would I go about doing that? How did I get the body I'd always thought of as *me*? Some cosmic disturbance, perhaps. Maybe I just got lucky for once. But luck had run out. I had to act, even if any such action resulted in nothing. Nothing was a great teacher, an imponderable but astute motivator. Nothing was doing a good job in educating me as to what I was now, so I might as well go looking for some type of replacement.

I traveled to a hospital, venturing carefully into the maternity ward. Quite a few babies were there, enduring a life-debut, and I was drawn to them. I was impressed with the little bundles, some sleeping, some wriggling. New lives! Just starting out on the hopefully long journey to old age and infirmity. New lives. Mostly blank slates, I supposed. Who remembers being a helpless infant? Helpless. Start over again in a new body, unable to take care of myself, dependent on others for my every need. Grow up and go back to school. Then work. Relationships. A mortgage. Arguments. I'd been through that before. I didn't think I could embody such a human life again, despite the brief intervals of joy and wonder. And what about a baby's soul? Did they have one? Could I share it? It didn't seem fair to either of us. There had to be another way.

I remembered reading that some Eastern philosophies claimed that you could sometimes be reincarnated as an animal, if there was some need or deed that you didn't attain in your previous human life. You could serve out the term of your animal life in order to receive the enlightenment you had detoured around before your last death.

It was an intriguing thought. If it were possible, what sort of animal would I want to be? Would I even have a choice, or would I get assigned a certain form depending upon my just-finished existential report card? When I was a child, my family always had a dog. I loved them. Dogs didn't seem to have a bad life. Except for the ones locked up in a diseased kennel, abandoned and awaiting euthanasia.

Well, there were horses, cows, and pigs. Tigers, leopards, and cougars. I put the thought of the amoeba out of mind. A tiger. Too large. But feline sounded good to me. Cats. I'd adopted numerous cats in my former life. I learned to respect their intelligence and value their companionship.

A well-cared for house cat, kept indoors, pampered and loved. This seemed like an accommodating choice. A good, cozy life filled with play and rest. But how could I make sure, if this was my goal, that I ended up in a good home with kind, understanding and patient humans? It wouldn't do to get kicked about. I'd have to be very observant. I couldn't let myself be taken home by just *anybody*.

Making this decision was easy. It was almost too easy. The thought of *cat* came to me without any firing of neurons in my phantom brain. I was just thinking that I was thinking. I felt a pull, as if I were being coerced into this; as if my "thoughts" were guided by some loftier ectoplasm that I couldn't grasp. This pull toward *cat* grew stronger.

It was no longer a pull. I was being dragged, compelled. Where before I could just imagine a place and go there, I suddenly found myself drifting away quickly and without my permission. I was fearful and tried to wrest back control, but it was useless. I was going somewhere and there was not a damned thing I could do about it.

I was like a child's balloon on a string. Tethered. The child running, the balloon playing catch up within the wind's gentle breath. I noticed little of my surroundings; I passed by too quickly, too oblivious to capture attention. I felt the earth tilt. That was all. And here I was.

Here was an animal shelter. Just the thing I was hoping to avoid.

Fleas. Ticks. Disease. Mange. Euthanasia, a fancy word for killing, meant to make us feel less queasy about the prospect of the death of those we neglect. But then, having died at least once, what did it matter? Fortunately, this place was clean. The dogs and cats looked healthy and happy, if lonely.

Now to find just the right kitten to become. I wondered how much of "me" I would still be when I became a kitten. I say *when*, but the question was really *if.* Here was the turning point of what was left to me. I knew it. I was being told the fact. I didn't know what would happen if I refused. I might finally end. That thought, I admit, appealed to me. Then again, a new experience would be welcome. Either way would be a relief from the wispy existence I now possessed. Part of me felt like letting go. But I couldn't. Not yet. I had to go further. I had to know. Something depended on me. It was the first real affirmation I'd felt since I died. I had to go through with it.

I'd have to really *be* the kitten; not a spectator, but a participant. I hoped that I'd still be able to think and reason and have my human memories intact as a cat. This plan would fall apart quickly if I couldn't. I had no memory of having done this sort of thing before, so I acted purely on instinct; that and the cosmic morality—or whatever brought me here—for an obviously structured, but undisclosed purpose.

My will to move about on my own returned. I floated past the cages of cats and kittens, looking closely at each one. I went down the line and then back again. Then I felt a …tickle. A rub in the fabric of creation. I was drawn to one particular cage that housed a cute grey and white kitten. I knew this was the one. It was a female, but that didn't seem to matter to either of us.

She was quite willing to share her body with me. She seemed to be expecting me and her eyes said, *"What took you so long?"* I became the kitten. I was still me, but now I was also kitten. It was quite confusing to the entirety of the me that remained so I let the kitten's little spirit take care of most of the operation of the kitten body. She knew what needed to done to stay alive. Gradually we merged, cooperated and became one entity. I had to set aside much of what I knew, but that was fine with me. I no longer needed it.

My new life was much simpler, more basic, more moment-to-moment than my human life had ever been. It was just what I wanted. I began to groom myself, waiting for the man to arrive.

Chapter Four

A Grudging Adoption

Edward Vorbec walked down the street, mumbling through the pain. His legs hurt. His back and hips frequently shot a bullet of agony up his spine. He was almost stoic about this. He was used to it. He had pills to relieve the suffering, but rarely took them anymore. His slippers made a slight *shoosh shoosh* sound as he slowly made his way to the animal shelter.

"Damn you, Cat," he muttered, drawing some suspicious looks from other pedestrians. "Another cat. At *our* age! Just what I needed…" Luckily, there was a shelter not far away from his home. It was, in fact, the same shelter where Bwca had adopted him so long ago that he barely remembered—and often regretted, in a strange and wistful manner.

The shelter was nine blocks away, but Mr. Vorbec was determined to walk every step. He could have taken a cab, but he was far too stubborn to entertain that idea. He'd by god walk while he still could, he thought to himself. He hadn't brought along a cat-carrier. That was something else he'd have to purchase, if he bought a cat. Then he'd have to take a cab back home. He was beginning to have second thoughts about the whole thing.

"Ridiculous!" he exclaimed. "Nonsense!"

These two words brought him more disapproving looks and even a few angry glares. Stupid old man. Probably crazy, said the glares. "What of it?" replied Mr. Vorbec. He knew what they were thinking. He had the advantage of the elderly: he didn't care at all. His life was mostly in the past now. Gone. Even memory was vaporized. He had the present, today—that and his demise. He didn't much care about the latter either.

It seemed he'd been walking all day, although he'd started out early. He hated being late and refused to wait in any line. By the time he arrived at the shelter, it had just opened for the day. Mr. Vorbec didn't go in. He slumped against the brick wall of the building and panted. "Catch my breath," he whispered and then let out what started as a chuckle, but turned into a cough. "Catch my breath, because it's running away. Heh. *Sonofabitch.*" He cleared his throat, pulled upon the shelter's door and entered.

The first thing that greeted him was the shelter's mascot, an African Grey parrot. It squawked at him, giving him a start. He stared at the bird. "Polly want a poisoned cracker?" he asked with a grin.

"Screw you," replied the parrot. That's what Mr. Vorbec heard in his own mind. The bird had actually said "Who knew?" It was as if the bird had been waiting for the old man to show up, so it could display a dollop of sarcasm.

"Bird stew," whispered Mr. Vorbec. There. He had the last word. The parrot squawked again, but that didn't count. He could now begin his search for the new cat. He had no idea why he had agreed to look at one, but thought he'd better get it over with. He had other, more important, things to do. He was left alone by the attendants as he made his way down the row of caged felines. Some of the kittens, and even the adult cats, shrunk back into the corners of their wire dwellings at his approach. A few mewled. One playfully pawed at him through the mesh. A couple were indifferent to his presence. Mr. Vorbec frowned. "Lots of cats needing homes." He made his way to end of the row, paced back, looked at the parrot, who has preening itself.

"Oh well. I tried, Cat. Wasn't meant to be."

As soon as he'd uttered these words, he experienced what he could barely consider a premonition of sorts. He'd never had such a thing, so he could only silently declare his sanity. But he was certain he heard a voice invade the suburbs of his mind. *Not a very good attempt, Vorbec. Go back. Go further. And this time, look, feel, know.*

The old man sighed. "Alzheimer's. Thank you, life." Against his better judgment, he began his second journey amongst the cats. It was no different than his first effort. Same cats, same reactions. Except for one grey kitten he hadn't recalled seeing before. It was curled up in a ball, sound asleep. He tapped on the cage. The kitten opened its eyes, yawned and stretched. It then approached the old man, whose face was now right up against the cage.

When it had gotten about a finger's length from the man, it sat down, cocked its head slightly, as Bwca had previously done, and just looked at him. Was the damn thing smiling, Mr. Vorbec wondered?

"Well?" The kitten yawned again, then resumed its study of the man. "Don't use up your entire vocabulary all at once," said Mr. Vorbec. The kitten retained its silence. "Meow? Surely you know that one. Fetch? Catnip, ball of yarn, flavor of the month? See a man about a horse and get your cakes baked brown?"

The kitten just looked…concerned. Mr. Vorbec was concerned about the kitten's look of concern. "Well, Quint, at least you won't talk me to death."

Quint? Where the hell had that name come from? Mr. Vorbec checked the tag on the cage. All that was written was "Female grey and white cat. Approximately 5 weeks old." No name. How strange, the old man thought. But then, what wasn't strange about this topsy-turvy day? Mr. Vorbec grinned back at the kitten.

"Quint, is it? Well, one thing's for certain. You'll outlive me."

Chapter 5

Homecoming

The ride from the shelter wasn't too bad, though toward the end I began to get a bit queasy from the motion of the taxi. I could only see out of the wire mesh door at the front of the carrier, so I had no idea where we were going. The man had put the carrier on the seat with the door facing him. If I put my eye right up against the mesh, I could see his face. He didn't look at me, he just stared straight ahead. I knew that this was the man I was supposed to adopt, and he was taking me somewhere, but he sure didn't seem very friendly. And why had he called me *Quint*? Was that my name now? This "becoming a cat" process had been quite overwhelming for the most part. Still, I was glad to be out of the cage at the shelter and going somewhere.

About the time I thought I was going to puke all over the inside of the wobbly box, the taxi stopped. The man paid the driver and then picked up my carrier and started walking. He was mumbling something. I couldn't quite catch all that he said, but I distinctly heard him say, "Damn you, Bwca. What have you gotten me into?" Who was *Bwca*? I saw a flight of steps ahead.

We went up the steps and into the building. He brought me down a dimly lit hallway and then set me on the tattered straw mat next to a dark brown wooden door. The carpet in the hallway smelled like moss and grass-cuttings. I heard the rattle of keys and then the man grumbled, "Damn shaky hands." Apparently he was having trouble getting the door open. When he finally managed to get the key to turn, we went in and he set me down. From what I could see, I was near an old worn armchair. There were some marks down low on the chair as if something had scratched at it or clawed it. I could smell old dust and something else. I let myself sink deeper into my cat self and recognized the smell as that of another cat. I looked a little closer at the carpet in front of me and saw that there were quite a few black hairs there. Other than at the shelter, this would be the first cat I had met in this body. I found that I was a bit nervous about the prospect. At the moment, though, I was stuck in this box, so whatever was going to happen next was beyond my control.

I heard the door close and the man grunt. I couldn't see the door. I could only see the armchair and the legs of a little table next to it. I heard a distant thump and then the man said, "I hope you're happy, Cat. I brought you a playmate." Was this "Cat" the "Bwca" he had been muttering about in the hallway? And then there he was, pure black. The other cat. He walked around my carrier and then looked in through the wire mesh. He had golden eyes. I cocked my head to acknowledge his presence and fell into his eyes. It was like nothing I'd ever experienced. I had fallen into another universe for a moment. Yes, this was Bwca. It wasn't at all frightening or overwhelming; it was where Bwca lived, and for just a second or two I lived there too. And then we were just two cats looking at each other. Bwca's head disappeared. I could still see his body. I crept up to the front of the carrier. Bwca was looking up at something.

"You want me to let her out?" asked the man. "Alright, but she's your cat, not mine. You're responsible for her."

I heard the man's footsteps on the carpet and then saw his hand work the mechanism that opened the carrier door. As it swung open, I bounded out. I let myself be the cat, completely. I scampered all over the place. There were just three rooms. I jumped up on the bed and then down. I rolled in the dust underneath the bed and ran back into the living room. I ran into the bathroom and jumped in and out of the tub. There was a tray in there full of cat litter. I paused for a moment and then spent some time digging and scratching and neatening up the mess. I ran back into the living room and made a sliding trip through the little kitchen that was open to the living room. I got a bit ahead of myself and rolled across the living room rug coming to rest against Bwca.

"Sorry," I warbled, without really thinking about communication or language.

"No problem," said Bwca.

I stopped, backed up three steps and sat down, astonished yet again.

"We can talk?"

"Obviously."

"Cats can talk? I didn't know cats could talk."

"Some are better at it than others. Some of us are more than cats."

"Can he understand us?" I looked up at the man.

"Sometimes. Not now, though. His name is Vorbec. Edward Vorbec."

"Vorbec. He's watching us."

"Not for long. Wait."

"You cats get out of the way now," said Mr. Vorbec as he walked over and picked up the carrier. "Where am I going to put this infernal thing?" He shuffled off toward the bedroom with the carrier in his hand.

"See how he is?" Bwca remarked.

"I noticed that he was kind of grumpy when he picked me up at the shelter."

"He's not very friendly," replied Bwca, "but he takes good care of me, and he'll take good care of you, too, if you treat him right."

"How is it that we can talk? I still don't get that part."

"Now is not the time for that. First you need to know the rules here."

"Rules? What rules? I'm a cat."

"Are you?"

Bwca looked at me again and I fell right back into his universe of other-than-cat substance. He was more than he appeared to be, bigger somehow, deeper, and old. Very, very old. This time I was afraid. Afraid I would be lost there forever. But then Bwca was present again, right there beside me and it was all right.

"What are you?" I asked.

"I'm just what you see, if you look at me the right way."

"You mentioned rules," I said, changing the subject.

"That I did, Quint."

"What's with calling me 'Quint?' The man, Vorbec, he did that, too."

"That's your name. Don't you remember?"

"What are you talking about? Remember what?"

"Let's talk about the rules. Come over here by the window. We'll speak in this lovely sunbeam."

I followed Bwca across the living room to the place on the floor where the sun was shining through the window. It was warm. Cozy.

"Rule number one," said Bwca, "is that you must always

behave as a normal cat would behave. Lie down there. I'll lie here next to you and explain it to you.

"I know who you *are*. I know who you *were*. In this life, you are a cat. You are also something beyond that. You are here for a reason . . ."

It was warm there in the sunbeam and I'd had a very long day. I drifted off to sleep as Bwca described how things were to be and told me what I needed to know. At least, I think I was asleep. When I woke up, I was more comfortable in my new body. I knew what to do and how to behave. I hopped up on the windowsill and watched a pigeon down on the sidewalk. I hadn't stopped wondering what Bwca really was, but I knew now that he would tell me when I was ready to listen. Right now, my job was to establish myself as part of the household, to make friends with Mr. Vorbec if I could, or at least to get him used to having me around. Bwca warned me not to expect too much from Mr. Vorbec right away.

I immersed myself in my new role. I scampered and leaped. I climbed the curtains. I knocked things off of the table and batted them all over the apartment. I hid things under the bed and then found them again later. I waited until Mr. Vorbec was sitting in his chair and then I would bat a toy into the living room and roll around playing with it. Then I would curl up and take a nap right next to his chair.

From across the room, Bwca looked at me and nodded his approval.

Chapter Six

Sarah

Mr. Vorbec watched Quint chase Bwca into the bedroom and then back again. He was in his armchair reading the newspaper, but he was also peeking at the playful cats. He feigned disinterest, but he found himself tolerably amused. His attention wandered back to the newspaper. He liked to keep an eye on the obituaries. Most everything else was a waste of ink to him. He went back to perusing the photos and the brief biographies of the recently dead.

The noise of the romping cats faded from his consciousness. He'd been surprised at himself by how quickly he'd gotten used to it—especially since, for the first few days, he toyed with the notion of taking both cats back to the shelter and have done with them once and for all.

He was reading about a Korean War veteran, who was survived by so-and-so, when Quint suddenly leaped upon his lap, her fuzzy tail flipping one side of the newspaper from his hand. Quint was just passing through, running from Bwca, who had been chasing her. But now Bwca stopped in mid-stride, sat down and looked at the telephone.

I sensed that I was no longer being chased and slid to a stop across the floor, turned and bristled. I looked to Bwca for guidance. What was going on? We'd been having so much fun! Bwca just stared at me and then turned his head back to the phone. I watching him intently.

The telephone rang.

"Damnation!" growled Mr. Vorbec. He tossed the newspaper aside and it fluttered to the floor like a bird's obituary. The old man rose slowly from the chair, walked to the stand, picked up the receiver and bashed it back into its cradle. It had rung four times before he could get to it. This was not merely unacceptable, this was a colossal insult. He paced back and forth, cursing the phone, muttering, spittle dripping from his withered lips.

I looked at Bwca, perplexed and frightened at the old man's behavior. I looked at Bwca for some sort of reassurance. "What just happened?"

Bwca merely opened one eye larger than the other, a kind of raising an eyebrow expression. Then he turned away and lay down sadly on the windowsill.

At the other end of the line, nearly a thousand miles away, a young lady gently put another receiver back onto the wall mount as her eyes welled with tears.

"Trying to call your grandfather again, Sarah?" asked the man who had just come into the room.

Sarah brushed her long auburn hair back with one hand, without turning around to face her husband. She wiped the tears away with her other hand.

"Christ, Sarah. You can't keep doing this to yourself. He's never going to forget or forgive. There's just no reaching him."

"I know. I know, Paul! If I could just talk to him, just once.

Explain why it happened and why he's so wrong."

"He's already decided he'll never get over it. You know how he is."

"I just can't let go, Paul." Sarah began to sob.

"Look, we've been over this. A dozen times. Honey, it's got to stop. He's determined not to talk to either of us." He put a comforting hand on his wife's shoulder. "You're just torturing yourself. I hate to see you like this…"

Sarah covered Paul's hand with her own.

"I'm worried about you, Sarah."

"I'm worried about *him*, Paul! He's eighty-seven years old and living so far away. So alone! What if he falls or gets sick?"

"Well. As long as he keeps hanging up on you, he's okay."

"That's not funny. That's just…mean." She removed Paul's hand from her shoulder and turned to face him. "He's my only living relative and it's stupid! It scares me that I'll never…" Sarah's face turned red and she began to weep. She pushed her husband away when he tried to embrace her.

"I'm not so sure anymore, Sarah. This thing with Ed has changed you. You can hardly think of anything else anymore."

"What am I supposed to think about right now?" asked Sarah, wiping away the tears that had turned angry.

"Us. Ed is destroying you. And me. And you're letting him do it!" He turned away himself and stopped short of walking out of the room.

"You know I love you, Paul. But I love him too. You've got to be with me on this." she pleaded.

"I'm trying, for Christ's sake." He shrugged his shoulders in resignation.

"What are we supposed to do? We can't force him to answer the damn phone. He's not senile. If he wanted to talk, he'd bloody well talk. You know that. And he's been pretty damn clear about his feelings. I don't know what else we can do!"

"I'm going to go see him."

"Sarah, for God's sake! Just listen to yourself! He doesn't want that!"

"I don't care what he wants. I'm going to go see him." She gave her husband a piercing look. "And you're coming with me."

Paul opened his mouth, but Sarah stopped him with a raised hand.

"Don't argue with me about this. Just book a flight. And hope that we get there in time."

Chapter Seven

Learning

"You're doing quite well, Quint," Bwca told me. "Vorbec is intrigued by your antics. As he starts to reach out to you try to touch his mind."

"When he tries to pet me? Is that what you mean?" I asked.

"That too, but it's more subtle than that. He longs for companionship, though he can't admit that, even to himself. He thinks he's beyond needing any other living creature. You have to gently encourage that need, let it draw you to him and him to you."

"Sometimes I can see that in his eyes, but then he looks away, looks inward."

"Work on extending the moment when you see that look in his eyes. Don't stare at him. Just draw him out very, very slightly, a little bit at a time. If you feel the pull at all, you're doing it wrong, you're too intense. Take your time. Patience is the key here. Like waiting for the right moment to pounce when hunting, you have to be ready and alert. If you move too quickly, or too soon, you miss your mark. It's all done with the eyes and the ears and, of course, the spirit."

Bwca showed me exactly what he meant, and then he and I practiced each day in the sunbeam. I used what I learned from Bwca with Mr. Vorbec. I was careful and deliberate and still I made mistakes. Sometimes I went at it a little too intensely and let the pull become too strong. Mr. Vorbec would get angry then.

"What are you doing, Cat? Leave me alone! Go play with that other cat. Go on! Get out of here!" he shouted and then added in a low, rumble, "Losing your mind there, Vorbec? It's a cat, remember?"

So, there were setbacks. Mr. Vorbec was unapproachable for days after he had gotten angry like that. It didn't matter what I did, how cute I was, what charming little sounds I made: whenever he saw me, he shooed me out of his sight. If Bwca hadn't been there to encourage me, I think I would have given up. You just can't communicate with an angry man. Try it sometime for yourself. They just don't listen.

Bwca helped in other, more direct, ways. He would trot into the room and lie down near where Mr. Vorbec was sitting, fuming and burbling in his chair. He'd lie down with his back to Mr. Vorbec and pretend to ignore him. Sometimes Mr. Vorbec would vent his rage to Bwca's back. That helped, Mr. Vorbec. It didn't help Bwca, though. Taking on all that anger was hard for Bwca. It takes a great effort to dissipate that sort of ugly, discordant energy, to soak it in and not turn it back against the sender. I couldn't do it, though I tried. Mr. Vorbec's anger drove me from the room every time. I don't know what it cost Bwca to endure that malignant energy, but there was a price and Bwca paid it. After absorbing one of Mr. Vorbec's tirades, Bwca came away sad and exhausted. I did what I could to help, but it was Bwca who had to get through it on his own. I just wasn't strong enough, or tough enough. I couldn't do it.

Days later, when Mr. Vorbec's anger had drained away, Bwca rested and I cautiously and carefully resumed my part of the task. I learned just the right moment to break away. I learned the power of just being in the same space with someone. There is a difference between being alone in a room and having a companion. I used that. I would go into the living room and warble a greeting at Mr. Vorbec and then lie down somewhere where he couldn't quite see me. Sometimes I would let my tail give me away, or my whiskered nose, or pair of crossed paws. I made him look for me. At times I would lie down right next to his armchair. All he had to do was look down over the arm to see me. When he did that, I would always look back up at him, hold his eyes a moment and then put my head down on my paws. I would sit on the window sill across from his chair and lash my tail back and forth.

"What do you see you out there, Cat?" he would ask.

I would turn my head to catch his eyes and then twitch my ears toward the sound of his voice. Once, he got up from his chair and came over to the window to find out what I was looking at.

"What's out there, Cat? I don't see anything. Was there a pigeon?" he asked and scratched me behind the ears. I pushed my head against his hand as a sign to continue. He looked down at me and said, "Huh," in a puzzled sort of voice, as if he had finally realized that I was there. As Mr. Vorbec turned and went back to his book and his chair, I saw Bwca in the bedroom doorway watching us. *Nicely done.*

Bwca and I continued our lessons in the sunbeam classroom. We moved on to more advanced subjects now that I had learned to apply the earlier ones. Sometimes I could get Bwca to tell me a little bit about who he was, but never all that much and not very often. What I did learn about him was hard to understand and some of it was hard to believe. But then, there were days when

I found everything that I was doing rather unbelievable. And there were moments when I would remember my previous life and the wonder of what I had become would overwhelm me. My thoughts would spin and spin, faster and faster, then slowly settle back down.

"Bad dream there, Cat?" Mr. Vorbec asked.

I was startled awake and for a moment I had no idea where I was. I frantically looked around. There was Mr. Vorbec, down on his hands and knees, his face inches away and displaying a look of concern that I had never seen before. With a long, boney finger he rubbed me behind my right ear in just the right spot. I looked up into his eyes. He turned away.

"Happens to me all the time," he said.

What? Bad dreams? He has bad dreams? How strange that he would say that to me. How unlike him. This was something new. I went back to my nap. I couldn't immediately go find Bwca and tell him about this unexpected development. It wasn't what a cat would do.

Sometime later, Bwca joined me on the window sill. "You've done something that I wasn't able to do, Quint. You've touched his heart. I'm very proud of you."

"Is that what it is? I guess you're right. It's certainly something unique for Mr. Vorbec."

"I think it will make all the difference needed."

"Really? But you did it, Bwca. You made all this happen."

"No, you did it, Quint. You went where I couldn't go. I just showed you the way."

"What happens now?"

"You just keep going. Slowly, carefully. Now is not the time to overreach. Back away a little bit, make him reach toward you. Be patient, be gentle. You are teaching him, Quint. And finally, finally he is learning."

Chapter Eight

Invocation

The very next day, Mr. Vorbec paced around his apartment, his hands clasped behind his back. He was full of thoughts. Odd thoughts. Memories and dreams. At times he seemed to be unable to distinguish between the two. It was a soupy disaster in his head. He knew he was awake. He was nervous. Hell, Mr. Edward Vorbec did not get apprehensive—at least not to this extent. Something didn't feel right. Something was just plain... wrong. He couldn't discover the error of this day. He could not pin down the ache that troubled him. It wasn't a physical pain. It was more like a rift in his soul, the kind no bandage or pills could treat.

"I wonder what those damned cats are getting themselves into?" he wondered. He hadn't seen them after he'd had his lunch. Not that it mattered. At least they weren't underfoot. He felt a twinge of regret about even having them in his apartment. Such a nuisance. A bother. He didn't need to be bothered anymore. He just needed to be left the hell alone.

He looked at the carpet, now even more frayed since he'd

brought the kitten back here. And yet he was interested in that kitten, despite himself.

Or perhaps *to* spite himself. Still, he'd smiled at Quint's silly antics. Why? "Silly" was certainly not in Mr. Vorbec's vocabulary. Hadn't been for more years than he could recall.

"What is it about that stupid kitten? Quint, eh? And the older one? Doesn't matter…" But the absence of the felines plagued him in ways he tried desperately to put out of his thoughts. "Here, there. It's all the same. No doubt they are off shredding something important to me. No matter. No matter at all." But it did matter. The old man began to pace again. "Now, if they were catching some filthy rodent… Bwca! Where the hell are you?" Damn. He had to stop this! It wasn't like him to care about cats. Or even rodents. He'd never notice if some tiny mouse happened to flitter about. Small things. Unimportant.

As soon as Mr. Vorbec said it, Bwca knew that it was time. This is what he'd been waiting for, working toward. For Bwca's name was more than a name, it was a summons that once invoked could not be undone. Bwca knew what was wrong with Mr. Vorbec. It was the same thing Bwca felt. It was the beginning of the end, the end of days, the end of worrying, the end of pain. Oh, yes, Bwca felt it. Being a cat this time around he didn't manifest his pain in any way that would show weakness. It was instinct for a cat never to appear vulnerable lest another animal consider him prey. He wondered if, perhaps, Mr. Vorbec had waited too long. Wondered if either of them had the strength required to see this through.

"Quint!" said Bwca. "Do you feel it?"

"I feel something. It's Mr. Vorbec. Something is wrong, isn't it?" I said.

"Very wrong, little one. It is time, but you will have to help. I can't do this alone. I will need your strength. Even with that, it may not be enough. No, it has to be. It will be."

"What do you mean, Bwca? I don't understand."

"You've awakened him, Quint. Remember when I told you that you had

touched his heart?"

"Sure, I remember."

"Well, I should have said 'warmed his heart.' The tiny spark you kindled there has been growing ever since, and now it has burst into flame."

"Is that good? It doesn't seem good. Mr. Vorbec doesn't sound well at all right now. He sounds worse than ever."

"Easy, Quint, easy. It's okay. It's what I've been trying to do since I came here. You were the one who provided the spark. Now we have to control the fire, direct it, make it work for us and for Mr. Vorbec. This is the hard part. This is where I will need your help the most."

"What do you want me to do?"

"Look at me."

I was inside Bwca's universe again, as I had been the first day I came here. It was vast and very, very dark and I was afraid and then Bwca was there with me and I knew what to do and how to do it and why it must be done.

"You see now, Quint, what we have to do."

"Yes," I said, "I understand it now. It's really quite simple."

"That it is, Quint, but it is also horribly difficult not just to do, but to experience."

"We have to, though, don't we? At least you have to and I'll help. It's why you brought me here, isn't it?"

"Yes, it is. Let me rest a moment and then we'll proceed."

A larger question suddenly entered Mr. Vorbec's mind. He stopped pacing again and looked at his telephone. It hadn't rung today. Not even once. It always rang, Every Single Stupid Day. At least once before lunchtime. How could he have the satisfaction of nearly breaking the cradle when he slammed down the receiver if the damned thing didn't even have the decency to ring?

"God forbid!" he declared to the silent telephone. He angrily picked up the receiver and was greeted with a dial tone. He dropped the receiver, like a coin into a beggar's cup. He sat down in his armchair with a weary, painful groan and thought about getting straight back up and making a cup of tea. But he was too tired. He stared at the buttons of his vest, as if they were just sewn on a moment ago. When he looked up, he noticed that Quint and Bwca had entered the room. They sat side-by-side, directly across from him. Waiting. They'd been fed. Mr. Vorbec had seen to that. What did they want? The whole apartment was their playground. But they weren't playing. They didn't move at all.

"Well?" asked the old man.

Quint and Bwca continued to stare at him.

"What the devil do you want? Go on, get the hell out of here," he said, but without much conviction. Mr. Vorbec twisted in his armchair, trying to get comfortable. He was feeling a peculiar hurt that had nothing to do with his tortured back, his arthritis or his neuralgia. He was experiencing regret. It slowly came back to him. He rubbed his face. The cats waited.

"For God's sake, I guess we'll just sit here until Christmas." The cats swished their tails. "Well, suppose I tell you a story, then?" Quint and Bwca meowed in unison. Mr. Vorbec chuckled. "It doesn't make much difference. Nobody would believe me or the two of you. Then again, nobody will ever know about it."

Chapter Nine

Revelations

Quint and Bwca approached the armchair, paused, sat down again. Their attention was completely focused on the old man.

"All right then. Once upon a time I was actually married. My wife and I had one child. A daughter. We doted on her. Wife's been gone many years. Cancer. Anyway, the child. She grew up, as do they all, and got married her own self. That seems the way of human life." He paused, reflecting back on years gone by.

"Daughter married, as I said. Nice young fellow, he appeared to be. Good as any, I suppose. Decent sort. Good to me. Always remembered my birthday, even when everyone else forgot. Kind of him, I thought. No use for birthdays, but you get my meaning."

Here, Mr. Vorbec raised himself out of his chair. He winced and made his way to the kitchen. He put the kettle on the stove to make himself a cup of tea. He imagined when he returned, he'd be able to stop talking. The cats would be off again. He wouldn't have to remember any more. To his surprise, the living room remained the same. The cats hadn't moved an inch. He sat back down and took a brief sip of the hot beverage.

"Well, with the wife gone, I guess they worried about me. Kept in touch. Visited when they could. They got busy, like all young folk. Had a child of their own…" The old man set his cup down upon the side table. He spared a glance at the telephone. He didn't remember picking up the receiver and putting it back in its cradle. He looked at the cats, who had followed his eyes. They looked back at him again.

"Had a child of their own," he repeated, "a girl. My granddaughter. Time for me, not so much. Had their own family. I wasn't ever neglected, mind you! Kept in touch, the lot of us. Didn't live as close as I'd have liked, but still. Hell of a good time. Thanksgiving. Christmas. Even Halloween a couple of times." Mr. Vorbec picked up his cup and took another sip. "You wouldn't have believed Halloween. What do you know about it, anyway? But I knew. I watched the witches, ghosts and goblins come by. Saw a skeleton once. Little chap was wearing all black. Used masking tape to make his bones. Now that was a sight!"

The old man paused again to drain his cup, by now merely lukewarm.

"That was innovation, I tell you," he resumed. "Life wasn't so bad. I was starting to get old. Grandfathers do. But the girl, my granddaughter…"

Mr. Vorbec put a hand to his mouth and coughed. He noticed some dark phlegm in his palm, got out his handkerchief, wiped it away and stuffed the package back into his pocket.

"The little girl. Her name was…Sarah. Yes. She was called… Sarah." Quint and Bwca looked at each other.

"You see what is happening, Quint?" asked Bwca.

"Yes, yes. Dampen it down now. Don't let him burn out."

"I'm trying. It's very hard. Help me."

"I am. Oh, I see. Yes, all right. Here we go."

The old man saw the cats exchange glances. "You don't believe me?" he roared. "Then you can both go to hell." The cats were unmoved by this invective.

"What happened was this," continued Mr. Vorbec. "My own daughter and her husband had gone out for the night. Left little Sarah with a babysitter. Car accident. Both dead. Both just... gone. Just like that." He snapped his fingers to accentuate the point. A tear rolled down his right cheek. He didn't notice.

"Sure there was a funeral! What did you expect? I held little Sarah's hand and my heart cracked as she wept. I wasn't as old then as I am now! I was her only living relative and I took her in. Raised her. She was a good kid and I did everything I could to keep her that way. And I don't give a damn if you believe me or not! Who are you to judge me? Damn cats. Didn't I take you in as well? Cats? Hell..." Mr. Vorbec spat upon the carpet.

"What did I do? Why, I loved her. That's what I did. Raised her. I told you that already. She graduated a year early and went off to the University. Watched her leave. Drove herself in a car I bought her. She was only seventeen years old. Almost as old as you are now, Bwca. You'll feel it too, Quint. In due time. Age. Good for the young, or so I'd thought."

The two cats moved another step closer, but remained aligned and alert.

"Here am I, talking to two damned cats. I don't have any sense left in me. I'm either dead or crazy." Quint meowed. Bwca tapped his friend with a paw.

"Hush. I've got it under control," said Bwca.

"We almost lost him there. Are you okay?"

"I'm fine. Just let me lean on you and be quiet. I need to concentrate."

"She—I'm talking about Sarah, wasn't at that school for two months when she calls me on that same damned telephone over there. The one that keeps ringing for no reason. She tells me she's gotten married! That's right! At seventeen! And me not there and not knowing the bastard!"

The old man put his head in his hands. Looked up again.

"Met him once. One time. She brought him to the old house. I sold that house quick. But she brought him. Wanted him to meet me. Well, we met. I told her, told Sarah, that I didn't approve of him. Hell, I don't even remember his name. It wasn't important. To me, he didn't have one. I told her right in front of him! Ha!"

I looked at Bwca. "This is it, isn't it? This is the key."

"We have to be very careful now. Balance is everything. Give me everything you've got now, Quint."

"Oh. I'm supposed to care what the two of you think? And pigs are balloons and fill the sky, eh?"

"I can't do it. I'm losing him. He's too angry!" said Bwca.

"Yes you can. You have to. We have to. Let me lend you more strength."

"I'll try. I'm so tired. I'm afraid it'll take too much to hold him now."

"Do it, Bwca. Do it or die trying."

Mr. Vorbec took a deep, rattling breath and then let out a long sigh.

"What I did was, I told them both to get the hell out and never come back. Disowned them. Well, he wasn't anything, but I disowned *her*. Haven't seen nor heard from her since. Don't even know where she lives. Or if she lives." He looked again at the telephone, forlornly. Then he turned his attention on the cats.

"The End," he proclaimed.

The cats took another step closer and sat. Mr. Vorbec rose unsteadily from his armchair. He stumbled and knocked his china tea cup onto the floor, shattering it. He didn't mind.

"That's it. No more. If you desire to be further entertained, you can go tear something up. Cough up a hairball. Sniff yourselves. I'm not your three-ringed circus. Now, if you don't mind—and with your great sufferance—I'd like to get some air before nightfall."

Mr. Vorbec left his apartment. He went for a walk.

"That's it," said Bwca. *"We did it. He's open now. He's ready."*

"You don't look so good, Bwca," I said.

"I'll be okay now. I just need to rest for a while. I don't remember when I've ever been this tired."

Bwca curled up on the floor there in front of the old armchair and went to sleep. I sat there next to him. I wasn't tired, though I felt like I should have been. I had to put my mind in order, to understand what had just happened. Knowing what Bwca had done was one thing. Watching him, and then helping him do it, was quite another. I sat there for a long time letting it settle into place. Finally, I curled up on the floor next to Bwca.

Chapter Ten

Refunds Not Accepted

Mr. Edward Vorbec walked down the stoop of his apartment building, trembling. He could not deny the fact that he was visibly shaking. He knew he must have been afflicted by some sort of psychiatric fit, since he'd just spent the better part of an afternoon talking to two cats. And telling them a story that he'd never fully told himself. What the hell was happening to him?

He shuffled along, nearly tripping over a cracked bit of sidewalk. He wished he'd purchased the cane he'd long thought about. It really would be of inestimable help to him at this moment. He felt ill. He'd never been so dizzy. But then, what could one expect after telling such a story to a couple of animals? Yes, it was all true. It was the most bitter part of his life vomited out like a hairball, soiling the carpet of his being.

There was some bizarre courtesy involved in spilling his innermost guts to Quint and Bwca. The cats. His cats. *Dear God,* he thought, *have I grown so fond of them? Please let it not be so.* He blamed himself. He'd let the cats get too close to him. And yet... he was giddy. Still dizzy, nearly down the street now, but he was smiling. Absurdly smiling, like a schoolboy on a carousel. He'd forgotten his hat and the breeze tousled his long white hair. It was sweet. It was a caramel apple. It was a kite held aloft in a cerulean sky only by a boy's steady hand.

Mr. Edward Vorbec stopped. He held his arms wide. His head tilted back, he let the wind take hold of him, carrying him, caressing him and he was running through meadows, past barns and silos and hay bales and he tested himself by running faster and faster, with Quint and Bwca chasing after him.

Then he fell.

He fell from the sky, the balloon of his skin burst, the string of his marrow snapped. He fell far. He fell into the arms of his mother, the sod of the fairground, still wearing his masking-tape skeleton costume, dancing with the demure ghosts conjured by all the full moons of his life.

He fell over and lay prostrate on the sidewalk, not twenty feet from his apartment building. He breathed. But it was the breath of books, pages turning, full of mildew, smelling of musk.

"Hey, Mister," said the first man to kneel by Mr. Vorbec. "Are you okay?"

"Oh my God!" exclaimed a woman who had witnessed the man falling.

"What happened?" asked another.

"He just fell over," the first man replied.

"Some old geezer just dropped dead. Yeah. No shit. Right in front of me!" said a man into a cell phone, walking past the scene.

"Somebody call 911!" yelled a voice from the inevitable crowd. "He's breathing!"

"He's got a pulse, but it's weak," the first man told the onlookers.

Mr. Edward Vorbec, aged eighty-seven and ill for many years, lay on the sidewalk, surrounded by strangers, in and out of consciousness, smiling like a child lucky enough not to be caught with his hand in the cookie jar.

Chapter Eleven

Arrivals

It was eerily silent in the back of the taxi. It had been the same on the airplane. A long flight with minimal conversation. Small talk. It made the journey seem to take forever. Now they endured the last leg of this mute pilgrimage, together and yet so coldly alone.

"It's too late to turn back now," Sarah said. She was acknowledging Paul's unspoken doubts.

"I know that, Sarah, it's just…" *A damned waste of time and money*, he continued in his own mind. This entire trip had cost them a bundle. In this insane economic crisis that was going on all over the world, now they were even deeper in debt.

"Sarah," Paul began.

"Don't say it, Paul. It's not worth hearing again."

"Look. I'm sorry. I was just going to say that I don't think he'll turn us away. I mean, he won't turn *you* away."

"I'm sorry too." She took his hand as she watched the city go by. "But it's the two of us now. Has been for a long time." Paul squeezed her hand as the taxi approached the apartment building of her beloved, misunderstood and misunderstanding, grandfather.

Sarah and Paul walked up the steps, hand in hand. They paused on the stoop. Sarah suddenly felt like a vine, withering in the season's first frost.

Paul looked for a button to push, to let them in. Finding none, he opened the door. They knew he lived on the second floor. They knew his room number. Sarah had been keeping track of him.

Would he be home? Paul almost hoped he wasn't.

They walked up the steps and slowly, cautiously, made their way down the dimly lit hallway. Dusk was approaching and the sunlight was turning away. Sarah was holding herself back and Paul found himself pulling her to Mr. Vorbec's door. And there it was. And there they stood.

"It's her," said Bwca.

"Her? You mean Sarah? His Sarah?" I could scarcely believe it. "You spoke to her, didn't you?"

"Yes, it's her. And Paul. Come with me."

I followed Bwca to the door that led to the hallway and sat beside him there waiting.

The door had no peephole. Paul looked at Sarah. She was just staring at the door. Then she knocked softly. No answer, no sound from within. She knocked again, loudly this time. They were greeted with the sound of cats mewling. Nothing else.

"Cats?" said Sarah, astounded. "He doesn't even like cats!"

"Do you suppose we have the wrong room?"

"No, you don't," said a voice behind them. "Not if you are looking for that odd Mr. Vorbec." A heavyset, middle-aged woman, her hair in curlers, held up a set of keys and jingled them. "Who might you be?"

Sarah frowned. "I'm Edward's granddaughter," she explained.

"Do you know if he's at home?"

"Didn't know he had any family. Didn't seem the sort."

"We haven't seen Ed in years," Paul added. "There was an... argument." He wasn't sure why he'd just admitted that. It was partly because he wanted to know whatever this woman knew.

"No surprise there," replied the key-lady. "I can't count the times he cursed me. I didn't mind. Sometimes I ignored him. Or else gave back as good as I'd got." Sarah smiled at this. It was so like him. "I'm sorry to be the one to tell you. It was today he fell sick. On the sidewalk. Just keeled over. He's in the hospital now."

"Is he...okay?" Sarah and Paul had stepped back, stunned at this news. It was what they'd feared. They were too late.

"In the hospital is all I know. Alive, for sure. Take an asteroid to kill that man." The woman shook her head and jangled her keys again. "No offense meant, dear."

But Sarah wasn't even listening anymore. She turned to Paul and tried to speak. Paul had suggested having the taxi wait, just in case, but Sarah wouldn't hear of it. Now she was fraught with fear and guilt.

The neighbor with the keys looked at the two of them, in pity, and sighed. "Look here." She held up her key-chain. "I've got a key to the old man's room. God knows why, but he gave me his spare. I'll let you in. Some stuff you might want to take care of before you go off to the hospital. He's got a phone. I've heard him slam the thing down nearly every day for years."

She unlocked the door for Sarah and Paul. "If the phone's broke, you can use mine. I'll leave you be now. Right across the hall if you need me." She poked a thumb behind her and then turned away.

Sarah and Paul entered the apartment, closing the door behind them. They saw the armchair. They saw the old rotary phone, the receiver resting on the tattered carpet. They saw the broken teacup, the saucer on the side table. Here was the repository of an old man's life. All his dreams—or non-dreams—all of his mere existence had settled here, like coal dust in a mine shaft.

What kind of life had living like this bred in him, wondered Sarah. It seemed almost too simple. She sat down in her grandfather's armchair. It smelled of sweat, coffee, tea and dust. All of these odors had settled there, just like her grandfather had. She rubbed the palms of her hands across the chair's upholstered arms. She caught herself and stood up quickly. She had to get to the hospital immediately.

She looked for Paul, but saw instead two cats. One old, one a mere kitten. They were sitting on the windowsill, enjoying the last shard of a sunbeam and staring directly at her with wide, feral eyes.

Chapter Twelve

Reunion

"No animals in the hospital, ma'am," said the duty nurse in the ICU. Sarah set the carrier down and glared at her. There was no mistaking the determination in Sarah's eyes. There could be no misunderstanding her look of *don't get in my way, whoever you are. Not now. I'll walk right through you and never even think about it again.* The nurse's cheeks colored and she looked away.

"My grandfather is here. His name is Edward Vorbec. I mean to see him. Get his doctor here now. Please." The nurse paged the attending physician. Sarah bent down and whispered to Quint and Bwca. Then she stood up again, her arms folded, daring the nurse to speak. They didn't have to wait long for the doctor to appear.

"Hello. I'm doctor Selman. You are," he glanced down at his chart, "Sarah?"

"Yes, how is my grandfather?" The physician noticed the cat carrier. He glanced at the duty nurse, who shook her head. Dr. Selman got the message.

"Come with me," he replied. Sarah picked up the carrier and

she and Paul followed him to a private room. She could see her grandfather through the window, lying still in a bed. She was surprised that he wasn't connected to the usual spider web of wires. He must not be so ill after all.

"Your grandfather is dying. I'm so sorry."

"No! How? What?" blurted Sarah.

"He's had an aneurysm in his brain. He's probably had it for quite some time. It's not all that uncommon. It can be treated, if caught early. His has ruptured. This caused a subarachnoid hemorrhage. His brain has filled with blood. We think it started this morning and that's why he fell on the sidewalk this afternoon."

"But…well, can't you operate?" Sarah pleaded.

Dr. Selman sighed. "No. We can't. It's progressed too rapidly. And at his age…well, to be honest, he no longer has the will to live. I'm sorry. There's nothing we can do but make him as comfortable as possible."

Sarah began to weep and turned to Paul. He embraced her. "How long…"

"Not long. A few hours. He should be in a coma. We don't know why he's still partly conscious."

"I, we, have to see him now," said Sarah, letting go of Paul and picking up the cat carrier. "Now, please."

"Of course. Go on in. All…four of you," replied Dr. Selman, looking in at the cats. Bwca and Quint meowed plaintively.

"He's here. Nearby. He's dying. Hurry, Sarah. Hurry," Bwca and I chorused.

They filed into Mr. Vorbec's room as quietly as possible. Sarah sat the carrier beside the bed. "Grandpa?" Mr. Vorbec's eyes opened. Then they opened wider.

"Sarah? Is it really you?"

"Yes, Grandpa, I'm here."

"So you are. And there's…Paul. Damned family reunion. Some potato salad and we'd have us a picnic, eh?"

"Grandpa," began Sarah, "I…" But the old man held up his hand and then dropped it.

"Hell, Sarah. It's been a wonderful life. In its own way. Heh. I'm glad you're here, both of you. And I know what you want to say. I'm old. Terribly old. I know most everything, like all old folk do. I sure wish I had a cup of tea…"

Sarah bent down and kissed him on the cheek. Mr. Vorbec grasped her with both hands and held her close. "We both have regrets," he whispered. "I won't say I'm sorry, even though I am. I missed too much of your own life and I dwindled away because of that. Can't change any of it. Probably wouldn't anyhow. Too damned stubborn."

"That's one of the things I love best about you," Sarah whispered back.

"Well then, we're not so different, you and I. Except…"

"Except what, Grandpa?"

"You wouldn't believe it, but I lived with a cat. Got old… older with the damned thing. Bad enough, that. Then went and got a kitten. Not so long ago. A pain in the ass, the both of 'em."

"They're here, Grandpa," said Sarah, "They wanted to come and I brought them."

"Bought them? What did you buy, m'dear?"

"No. Brought. Your cats. Bwca and Quint." She bent down and opened the door of the cat carrier.

I leaped out of the carrier as soon as Sarah had opened the door. I settled on Mr. Vorbec's legs. I realized how thin he was, just skin and bones really. Bwca was too weak to stand. He looked up at Sarah. "Help me," he pleaded.

Sarah lifted him and set him upon her grandfather's mid-section. Mr. Vorbec raised his head slightly, just enough to see the felines looking at him.

"Oh hell no!" he exclaimed. "I was sure I made an excellent escape. Planned it out and all."

"No, you didn't, Grandpa," replied Sarah.

"I should have. Meant to." Mr. Vorbec's head sank back into his pillow. He allowed himself a little smile. He didn't think anyone would notice. Quint did. Bwca just curled up and closed his eyes.

"It's finished. We did it. Things are as they should be. Now I can rest," whispered Bwca.

"Bwca?"

"Thank you, Quint," he whispered.

"Well then," said Mr. Vorbec, his voice raspier. "What's next?" Sarah wasn't sure what he meant and didn't know how to answer. "You two," he explained. "You and Paul. Go make some babies. At least one. Drive carefully."

"What...Grandpa?" Mr. Vorbec's head had turned to the side. His breathing stopped. The heart monitor was singing a flat monotone. He was gone. Sarah began to sob, but not all the tears were from sorrow. She was grateful to have had these last few minutes with a man she adored. Himself to the very end.

She leaned over to pick up Bwca. To her surprise, Bwca was also gone. He'd died along with her Grandpa. "Oh!" she managed to utter. Dr. Selman had come into the room and applied his stethoscope to Mr. Vorbec's chest. Then, to his own astonishment, he did the same for Bwca. He pronounced them both dead.

"Again, I'm so very sorry," he said. "It was a bit of a miracle, really. Your grandfather shouldn't have been able to talk at all. Don't let it bother you if he didn't make much sense."

"He made *perfect* sense, Doctor," Sarah replied. "He was never better."

I looked up at Bwca and at Mr. Vorbec. Do cats weep? I can only speak for myself when I say that this one did. I mourned the loss of my teacher, my companion, my friend, Bwca. I understood why it had to be, but that didn't make it any easier. I knew what Bwca had done and why. And I knew what I was going to have to do. Without Bwca, it was going to be a much more difficult and lonely road to travel. For a moment, the weight of it crushed me. I gave myself wholly over to the heartache. It was all I could do to keep from crying out in misery. Sarah had to put me back in the carrier. I had no energy to move. Grief, for the moment, consumed me entirely.

Dr. Selman returned with some papers for Sarah to sign and asked about "arrangements." Before they left Mr. Vorbec's apartment, Paul had found his Last Will and Testament. Oddly, it was on the little table beside his armchair. His wish was to be cremated. Sarah asked that the bodies be taken to the funeral home listed in the will.

"What about the cat?" the doctor asked.

"They go together. In death as in life. Together. Whether they like it or not."

Chapter Thirteen

The Beginning

Sarah and Paul stayed in Mr. Vorbec's apartment, while they completed the relatively easy task of packing up his paintings and other artwork and putting his affairs in order. His Will had been short and concise. He left all his worldly possessions to Sarah, including—to her incredulity, the two cats. How mysterious it seemed to find that addendum in the Will. When had he done that? Why? He seemed almost indifferent to them in life. Obviously, he hadn't entertained the notion that Bwca would die with him. Quint spent this time sitting in the windowsill. She sometimes watched their progress, but seemed for the most part to be lost in her own world.

The sadness I felt was overwhelming. I sat on the windowsill, where Bwca and I had spent so much time together. I watched Sarah and Paul pack up Mr. Vorbec's things. Bwca's few things. Things. Reminders of their owners. Keepsakes to the living. I looked out at the austere, gray sky and the bleak, dark world. I curled up and sobbed myself to sleep.

There had been no real ceremony for Mr. Edward Vorbec and Bwca. They were cremated together. A rather nondescript

Urn, containing their intermingled ashes, was given to Sarah. She doubted that this was what her grandfather would have wanted. He probably would have preferred an old shoe box, but she didn't intend to let him off the hook so easily. The Urn was mostly for the sake of Bwca.

The day before their flight home, Sarah and Paul took a walk. Sarah wanted Paul to see the place where she and her grandfather had been happiest. It was a small park at the edge of a pond. Nearby stood the old playground equipment, still well-maintained. It had seemed so immense to her child self. Not much had changed. There was the merry-go-round, the teeter-totter, the monkey bars she could never quite reach on her own. There was also a cedar tree-house, set not too high off the ground. Just lofty enough to challenge the children who played here now. This was new. Sarah had an instant urge to explore it. Maybe later. There were other, more pressing urges calling to her.

Sarah and Paul walked along the pond's rim. Sarah held the Urn to her breast. Quint walked beside them, unfettered by cage or leash. They were amazed that she wouldn't rush off when she saw a bird or squirrel. She'd watch them, but she refused to give chase.

Sarah and Paul had taken me with them to the park. I guess they had become fond of me. Didn't want to leave me behind in that old, empty apartment. I walked with them through the park, sometimes following them, sometimes just walking alongside Sarah. I knew to keep close to them. I had no interest in chasing the birds or squirrels that inhabited the place. Not today. I just gave them a look that let them know I could run them into the branches if I chose to.

Sarah suddenly laughed.

"What's so funny?" asked Paul, stooping to scratch Quint's neck.

"Just a memory. A very dear one. This place brought it back." She giggled. "One day, we were about to go home. Back to the old home across town, long before he sold it. He just stopped in his tracks. I nearly ran into him. He turned and grabbed my shoulders. Spun me around. 'This!' he said.

I looked up at him. He was so tall. His arms were spread to the heavens. I remember thinking he might bring down some lightning on us. 'This will someday be yours! Vorbec's Park!' Then he took my hand in his and we left. I think he chuckled all the way home."

Paul snorted.

Sarah smacked his arm with a fist. "I'm serious! And so was he. I was a little bit scared and a little bit excited. It was weird."

"Sorry," Paul chuckled. "But he was a bit...well, crazy if you like."

"I did like. Do like. He was always larger than life in his own small way. It's no wonder I couldn't get him out of my head. And why I had to come back when I did. When *we* did." She looked down at Quint.

"His cat seems to take after him," Paul remarked. "It's eerie the way she just walks along with us. The way she refuses to stray..."

"Yes it is," mused Sarah. "Y'know, it's so comical. I mean, he was never fond of dogs, even when I was a child. He had no use for cats at all. He actually seemed to loathe them."

"Hmm. So we're stuck with this one, huh?"

"Or she's stuck with us. Come on. We're almost there."

The three of them walked on until they approached a large, rectangular sandbox. A plastic green pail was overturned near the center. A yellow shovel and fork had been left at the border.

"No. Wait a minute, Sarah" exclaimed Paul. "You can't be serious!"

"I can be, but I'm not right now," she grinned.

"Please," he implored. "Think about this. It's not sanitary!"

"Grandpa bathed. Bwca seemed clean enough. What more do you want?"

"Not to spread some sort of bacteria? Not to mention not getting arrested." Paul hastily looked around to see if anyone was watching them.

The park was deserted, the children called home to supper and television.

"You've been so lovely up till now, Paul. Don't turn into a shit."

Paul started to speak up, thought better of it and resigned himself to the inevitable. Sarah opened the Urn and dumped the ashes of Mr. Edward Vorbec, and the cat, Bwca, onto the sand. She picked up the little shovel and began to mix sand and ash. Paul sighed, grabbed the matching fork, and helped to stir the cauldron of man and cat into an inseparable stew of atoms.

Quint, who had been sitting placidly, grooming herself, jumped into the joyous fray, scratching, digging and clawing up whirlwinds of the stuff behind her. It was a glorious free-for-all.

When they were finished, Sarah and Paul stood up, sweating but satisfied. Quint still sat in the sandbox. She looked preoccupied.

"C'mon, cat," said Paul.

"Just a second." She looked intently at Quint. "We have time. Let her be."

They couldn't hear it. But I could. Bwca and Mr. Vorbec had stopped by to check on us. I was happy to know that Mr. Vorbec was in good hands. And I was comforted. I knew this was not the end. It was simply another beginning. And they were happening all the time, all around us.

"Did you see that?" asked Mr. Vorbec.

"Of course I did," replied Bwca.

Mr. Vorbec cackled. *"A helluva thing! A grand way to get sent off!"*

"*So it was,*" Bwca observed. "*We have to go now. Existence awaits.*"

Mr. Vorbec looked down at the cat. "*Maybe you don't get it, Bwca. I'm dead! And I'm not the only one, if you get my drift.*"

Bwca sighed. "*It's not the first time for me. Nor the last for either of us. Don't worry. I'll stay with you for a while.*"

"*I was afraid you'd say that. It just seems like a damned shame…*"

The conversation faded as the two of them moved on. I looked up to see Sarah and Paul staring at me. They seemed bewildered.

"*Time to go,*" I explained. What they heard was "*Miaow.*" We'd have to work on that.

Acknowledgements

Michael Titus

First of all, I need to thank my friend, co-author and fellow cat lover, Brett Fernau. For his "catversations," his wonderful, elegant ideas when I just wandered in the dark. For being a genuine and caring human being and a delight to collaborate with. Secondly, the inimitable and inexplicably brilliant Julie Miller for her generosity, her book design, her majestic and lovely book cover—and continued support. She is such a creative genius and it's comforting to have her in my corner. Other gracious support came from Jon Rogers and Zack Kay, when it was most needed. Finally, my family and my cats. Bwca and Quint are real. Bwca is gone now, but not forgotten. My thanks again to you, dear reader, for taking this journey with us.

Brett Fernau

Thanks to Michael Titus, whose post on Facebook was the nudge that put this whole project into motion. He is a pleasure to work with and his ability to create unforgettable characters is wonderful to behold. I am convinced that he and I must be brothers of different parents. I envy his toy collection and his ever-present spirit of play. I must echo Michael on Julie Miller's contribution to this book. She is an Artist. I can offer no higher praise to anyone. Of course, thanks to my wife, Carol, for putting up with me for the last 35 years. She has always been my biggest fan and my staunchest supporter in all my artistic endeavors. I can't imagine what would have become of me if not for her. Thanks to all the cats who have ever let me adopt them, especially Quint and Hedge who live with us now. You can live without a cat, but I'm not sure why you would want to. Finally, thank you for buying and reading this book. I hope you enjoy it as much as Michael and I enjoyed writing it.

Michael Titus lives with his four cats, including Bwca, who is a ghost, surrounded by the hauntingly beautiful mountains of rural West Virginia. He is fond of coffee and tea, and collects small tin wind-up toy robots and bowler hats. This is his second book. He still has many stories to tell.

corvidmuseum.blogspot.com
thegirlwhoreadtobirds.com

Brett Fernau is a photographer, writer, actor, musician, blogger and shade-tree mechanic who lives in Los Angeles with his wife, Carol, and their two cats. He loves to read and collect books of all sorts. He also enjoys restoring and driving vintage Volkswagens. When not otherwise occupied he likes exploring the public stairways which are hidden all over the city. He writes short stories about cats and publishes them as e-books. This is his first real book.

brettfernau.com

Cover illustration and interior design
by Julie Miller ~ HaggisVitae.com